One sunny afternoon, Brian was nibbling grass, minding his own business,

when...

along came another sheep.

"Hello," the sheep said. "My name is Rose."
Rose had **black** wool and curly horns.

meheheh!

"Hello," said Brian. "Let's be friends."
"All right," said Rose.

And they chased each other round and round the field and over the little hill,

baaaaah!

until...

along came another sheep.

"Hello," the sheep said.
"My name is Stanley."

But Stanley said,

"I only like sheep with **black** wool. White wool is rubbish. I am just going to play with Rose."

Stanley had **black** wool, but no horns.
"Hello," said Brian.
"Let's be friends."

So Stanley and Rose chased each other round and round the field and over the little hill.

They wouldn't let Brian join in.

Brian felt very sad.

Then along came another sheep. And another.

"Hello," the sheep said. "We're Tracey and Frank."
Tracey and Frank had white wool with big
black and yellow spots, and curly horns.
"Hello," said Brian. "Let's all be friends."
But Tracey and Frank said, "We only want sheep
who have horns in our gang."

Well, Brian had horns, so he was all right.
And so did Rose.
But Stanley didn't, so he wasn't allowed to join
Tracey and Frank's gang.

And that made *Stanley*
feel very sad.

Then along came another sheep.

And another. And another.

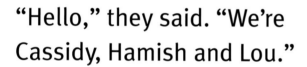

"Hello," they said. "We're
Cassidy, Hamish and Lou."

Cassidy, Hamish and Lou had
blue wool with pink stripes,
and no horns.

"Hello," said Brian. "Let's all be friends."
But Cassidy, Hamish and Lou said,
"We don't like sheep with white wool or **black** wool.
White wool and **black** wool are rubbish. We think..."

But Brian had had enough.

"We are all sheep," he told them. "We should all play together!"

And suddenly everyone started talking and laughing.

"Wahoo!" Brian cheered. "This is more like it!"

But then...

Rose gave Brian a funny look. "You've got blue eyes, Brian," she said.
"Blue eyes are rubbish," said Tracey and Frank.
"Brown eyes are best!" said Cassidy, Hamish and Lou.

"All those in the Brown-Eye Gang, follow me," said Stanley
(who should have known better).
And off they all went to chase round and round the field and over the little hill...

without Brian.

And Brian felt
very, very, very sad.

Brian left the others and walked away.
He came to a lake and looked at his reflection.
He looked at his white wool.
He looked at his curly horns.

He walked across a field,

up a big hill

and into a forest,
where he bumped into...

Brian turned round and ran as fast as his hooves would take him,

WOLF!

out of the forest,

WOLF!

down the hill,
across the field,
past the lake,

to warn the others.

WOLF!

The sheep ran this way.
The sheep ran that way.
The wolf ran after them.

Things were looking bad –

until...

Brian took charge.

"Sheep! Friends!

We can beat this wolf –
if we all work together!

ATTACK!"

The sheep with white wool
ran ahead.
The sheep with **black** wool
snuck up from behind.

The sheep with curly horns went

BIFF!

The sheep with no horns went

BUTT!

And the wolf ran away, and was never seen again.

"Hooray!"
cried the sheep. "We did it!"

They lifted Brian ^{high} up onto their
shoulders and carried him
round the field.

"Brian! Brian! Brian!"
they cheered.

But then Brian said,
"Just a minute. Some of you go *baaaaah!*

Some of you go *meheheheh!*

And ONE of you goes
baaa-carumbaaa!

And **I** think...

that's just FINE!"

And the sheep all chased each other round and round the field and over the little hill...

until it was time to sleep.